Anthony
Creepy Crawlies

LORNA AND GRAHAM PHILPOT

Random House 🏠 New York

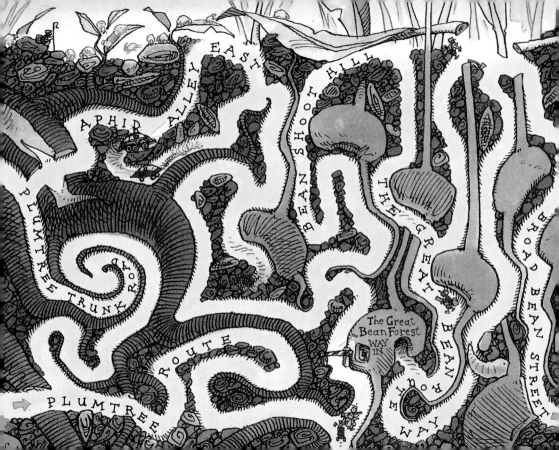

To/ Bobby Ant
Beanstalk Cabin
Leafcutter Lane
up Bean Route Way
The Great Bean Forest

AntMail

To/ Terry Termite
Termite House
10 Termite Terrace
down Bean Route Way
The Great Bean Forest

AntMail

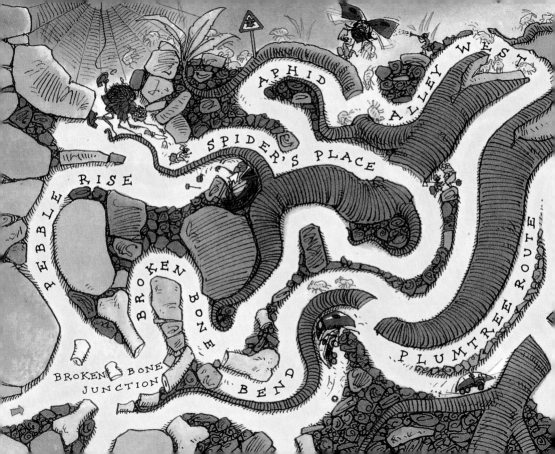